BEING BATMAN

Adapted by Michael Petranek

Based on the story by
Seth Grahame-Smith and the
screenplay by Seth Grahame-Smith
and Chris McKenna & Erik Sommers
and Jared Stern & John Whittington,
based on LEGO Construction Toys.

SCHOLASTIC INC.

10 9 8 7 6 5 4 3 2 1   17 18 19 20 21
Printed in the U.S.A.   40

First printing 2017
Book design by Jessica Meltzer

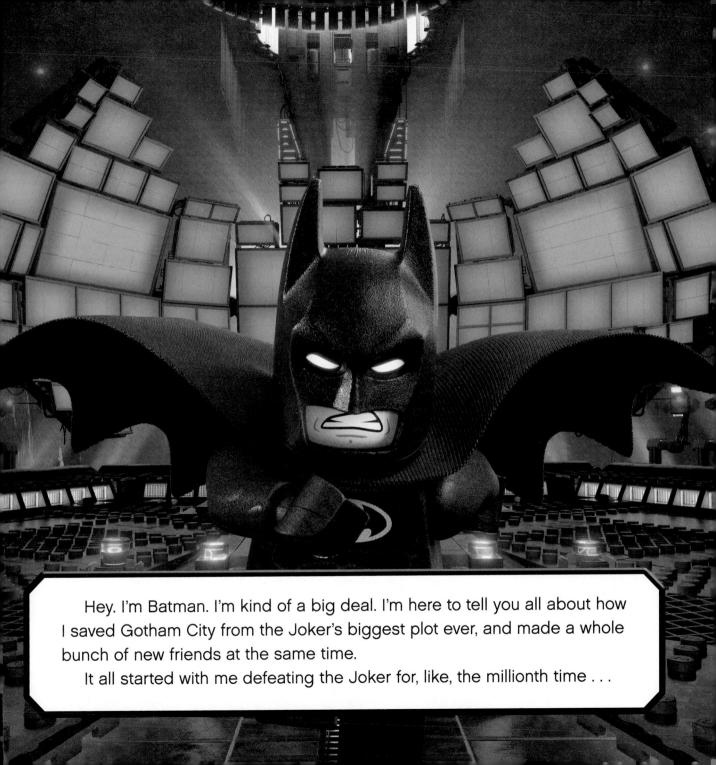

Hey. I'm Batman. I'm kind of a big deal. I'm here to tell you all about how I saved Gotham City from the Joker's biggest plot ever, and made a whole bunch of new friends at the same time.

It all started with me defeating the Joker for, like, the millionth time . . .

I had just caught up to the Joker when he told me I spent so much time chasing him, we were basically best friends.

I laughed. That's crazy, even for a crazy clown. "You're not my friend," I said. "You never have been."

He got away, but I totally saved the day.

Later that day, I saw Superman on the news. He had just sent his nemesis to the Phantom Zone using this fancy projector.

Superman said the Phantom Zone was a jail for the universe's most notorious bad guys.

Hmm . . .

That night, there was a big party for Gotham City Police Commissioner Jim Gordon. And at the same time, Bruce Wayne adopted a kid . . . kind of by accident.

Since I am Bruce Wayne, that meant I'd adopted a kid, too. Boy, was I surprised when Alfred told me I was a dad!

Then guess who showed up? The Joker! And he turned himself in! I knew he was up to something, even if no one else did. Don't forget—I'm Batman.

I also knew what had to be done.

When I got back to the Batcave, the new kid was there. He was really nimble, small, and quiet. He could totally help me borrow the Phantom Zone Projector from Superman!

But he needed a disguise. The costume was, uh . . .

Well, the kid really seemed to like it, so . . .

We snuck into the Fortress of Solitude and totally got the projector without anyone noticing!

At first, I wasn't sure how the kid would do. But actually, he turned out to be pretty helpful.

I went to the jail where the Joker was being held and totally zapped him.

Boo-ya! That's how you do it! Like a boss.

Our story should end here, but no . . .

The new police commissioner, Barbara Gordon, locked me in jail! Me! In jail!

Apparently, she was mad that I broke in and broke the law, which I guess I can see since she's the commissioner and all.

Barbara said that the Joker might have actually WANTED to go to the Phantom Zone. But that's silly.

I'm sure he didn't actually want to go there, but the Joker got a bunch of new powers in the Phantom Zone and took over Gotham City. He totally wouldn't have been able to do that if I wasn't locked in jail!

So Barbara came and got me out of jail. Turns out the city needed Batman, and she wanted me to work with her! Alfred and the kid were there, too.

I wasn't used to working with anyone else, but the kid said, "Just think of us as gadgets in your Utility Belt." That worked for me.

First, my team needed costumes. There were all officially representing the Batman brand. That means, always wear officially licensed Batgear, trademark Batman.

We hopped in my Batwing only to see that the Joker had totally taken over Wayne Manor and the Batcave! There was no way I could let this stand.

We had to make a, uh, creative landing. It turns out that the Joker had some tricks up his sleeve.

No biggie, though. I needed a new plane anyway. It's cool.

I had the team wait outside because I didn't want them to get hurt. But then the Joker played a supremely not-cool trick on me and caught me in his funhouse. "The Joker is your nemesis," he said. "You blew off your team, and you won't even admit we're total bros, friendos till the endos. We're nemeses!"

Before I could say anything, the Joker beamed me up into the Phantom Zone. It was totally cheating, because if he had given me time to say something, I would have had a great comeback.

It turns out there's a Warden in the Phantom Zone. She told me the key to defeating the Joker—teamwork. That's what I'd been missing this whole time.

The Warden sent me back, and I knew what I had to do.
I came back and I, uh, apologized to Alfred, Barbara, and the kid.
Then we all teamed up. Go, Bat-family!

We pretty much defeated the Joker right away, and he ran away to the Gotham City Energy Plant. He was done. Finished. And it was time for me to put him away for good . . .

Well, I would have. But I realized something: The Joker is the reason that I lift weights until my chest is positively sick. He's given me the best fights of my life. Because of him, I'm a better Batman. In a weird way, we kind of *are* friends.

When I told him that, he was pretty happy.

So what next? Well, we had to clean up the city. The Joker, uh, he broke, like, a LOT of stuff. It was kind of a problem, actually.

And that's it. I learned that with friends, you can pretty much accomplish anything. And I'm sure the Joker will be back to his old tricks in time. But for now, we're one big happy Bat-family and NOTHING is going to stand in our way!

© 2017 WBEI & DC Comics. © 2017 The LEGO Group. (s17)
ISBN 978-1-338-11817-9   PO 546243